Little Mook
AND
Dwarf Longnose

· Wilhelm Hauff ·

Little Mook
AND
Dwarf Longnose

Illustrated by

Boris Pak

Translated from the German by
Thomas S. Hansen & Abby Hansen
Preface by Thomas S. Hansen

qp

A Pocket Paragon Book

David R. Godine · Publisher

Boston

This is a Pocket Paragon Book
published in 2004 by
David R. Godine, Publisher
Post Office Box 450
Jaffrey, New Hampshire 03452
www.godine.com

Library of Congress Cataloging-in-Publication Data
Hauff, Wilhelm, 1802–1827.
[Kleine Muck. English]
Little Mook; and, Dwarf Longnose / Wilhelm Hauff ;
illustrated by Boris Pak ; translated from the German
by Thomas Hansen & Abby Hansen.— 1st ed.
p.   cm. — (A pocket parragon book)
Summary: Two stories in which disadvantaged characters
use magic to overcome adversity.
ISBN 1–56792–222–8
1. Fairy tales—Germany. 2. Children's stories, German. [1. Fairy tales.
2. Short stories.] I. Pak, Boris, 1935– ill. II. Hansen, Thomas.
III. Hansen Abby, J., 1945– IV. Hauff, Wilhelm, 1802–1827.
Zwerg Nase. English. V. Title. VI. Pocket paragon series.
PZ8.H293LK   2003
[Fic]—dc22   2003016063

First Edition
*Printed in China by Everbest Printing Co.
through Four Color Imports, Ltd.*

Preface

Wilhelm Hauff's life is a story of meteoric literary success and early death. Born in Stuttgart on November 29, 1802, in the south German kingdom of Württemberg, Hauff died prematurely from overwork and exhaustion on November 18, 1827, just short of his twenty-fifth birthday. During a brief and dazzling period of creativity, he wrote tales and novels that have remained in print through countless editions. Among German-speaking children, their popularity is second only to the famous *Nursery and Household Tales* of the brothers Jakob and Wilhelm Grimm, published in 1812.

Hauff was one of three children born to a prominent family of lawyers and civil servants loyal to the court of Württemberg. He prepared for university at the monastery school of Blaubeuren but left characteristically early to begin studying theology at the University of Tübingen. It was his intention to become a Lutheran pastor but, after entering university as a scholarship student in October 1820, he turned to literature instead. Inspired by the emotional politics of the day, he began to write patriotic verses. His older brother, Hermann, already a medical student at the university with connections to its fraternity, introduced Wilhelm to the club. In Hauff's time fraternities were not only dueling and drinking societies, but also politically tinged organizations with liberal leanings. Their members shared the idealistic objective of unifying the hundreds of small German-speaking principalities and kingdoms of the period into a single, constitutionally governed nation-state. Some fraternity members violently pursued their political agenda. Not surprisingly, their methods brought them under surveillance by the authorities.

It is difficult today to imagine the cultural significance that fairy tales possessed in the political climate of the first half of the nineteenth century when Wilhelm Hauff attended university. At the time the Grimms' collection appeared in 1812, an entire generation in the German states had known nothing but war with France – war that did not end until Napoleon's defeat at Waterloo in 1815. Readers and writers alike quickly romanticized German folk songs and fairy tales to represent an imagined past age of innocence and heroism before the feuding principalities and political turmoil of the Napoleonic wars existed. In their place, such texts portrayed an idealized, single German state. In fact, the reality of a unified German nation was not achieved until 1871. During Hauff's youth in post-Napoleonic Europe, this notion was still subversive and dangerous to express unambiguously.

After showing early enthusiasm for the radical cause of the German fraternities, Hauff distanced himself from the potential violence of the movement and dedicated himself to his studies. Once again he graduated early, leaving the university in 1824 with a doctorate in philosophy. After earning his degree, he spent his three remaining years in a powerful burst of creative energy. His first published work appeared anonymously, alongside works by other writers in an anthology of idealistic, patriotic poetry. The volume was released by a publisher in Stuttgart in 1824. It was at this point that Hauff postponed his plans to enter the ministry and took employment with a sophisticated, prominent family in the city of Stuttgart as private tutor for their two sons. During the two years that he held this position, Hauff gained social polish and contacts that helped spread his fame. He produced his first collection of stories in 1825 at the age of twenty-two, after having tested these tales on his two pupils, whom he took as his model audience.

In their content, settings, and style, Hauff's stories conjure up a different world from that of most German folk tales. To begin with, his stories do not convey their moral and cultural lessons with the starkly intimidating, often cruel imagery that distinguishes many of the Grimms' tales. Hauff's central figures are children of the Enlightenment, and his tales carry messages both educational in intent and, by comparison to much of the folk material, benevolent in tone. His settings are more exotic than those of the Grimms, and his characters have an intrinsic appeal that makes it easy for children to identify with their struggles against magical difficulties. Some of them – sympathetic figures from the Muslim world – were novelties to the German-speaking children of the time. Hauff seems to have lifted his characters straight from their bazaars and mosques, clad in colorful turbans and long beards, to present them on the stage of German literature. His depiction of Islam as a belief that guides wise sages and prudent rulers continues the tradition of religious tolerance that harks back to the Enlightenment. At the same time that Hauff embeds lessons of moral generosity in his children's stories, he also offers readers an imaginative escape from the everyday reality of their own domestic spheres, for despite the moral and social content in his tales, his primary goal is to entertain.

Thanks in part to the popularity of the Grimm brothers' work, Hauff had little trouble in quickly finding a place on bookshelves beside the famous *Nursery and Household Tales.* It is worth noting that the Grimms, although still perhaps the world's most famous collectors and popularizers of folk material, were not the first to publish fairy tales. Charles Perrault's compendium, *Contes de ma mère l'Oye* [Tales of Mother Goose, 1697], included the first published versions of "Little Red Riding Hood" and "Cinderella." The Grimms' collection of German material differed from its predecessors in that it was meant for a broad public, rather than just the cultivated elite. As a result, their stories easily gained immense popular appeal by virtue of their simply-told, archetypally timeless content and the additional revolutionary fact that they were addressed directly to children.

In his boyhood, Wilhelm Hauff was an enthusiastic and retentive young listener to this folk material. The talented lad absorbed the Grimm brothers' plots and motifs, and many of their themes surfaced later in Hauff's own contributions to the genre of the poetic art tale. Hauff wrote three such books of tales in the brief time that he lived after finishing his studies. In addition to *Lichtenstein* (1826), his famous popular novel set in the Middle Ages, and a couple of novellas, three collections of tales constitute the basis of his literary reputation. Their titles are: *The Caravan* (1826), *The Sheik of Alexandria and His Slaves* (1827), and *The Tavern in Spessart* (published posthumously in 1828). "Little Mook" is typical of the stories in the first of these volumes, which are all set in the Orient. The tales in the second volume (containing "Dwarf Longnose") have western as well as oriental settings. Hauff originally included texts by other authors, such as the Grimms, along with his own, in this collection. The third volume contains material set mostly in Germany.

Part of Hauff's enduring appeal is his ability to dress down-to-earth stories in colorful exoticism. As a result, they are anchored in a world markedly more material than the uncanny environments typical of German romantics like his older contemporaries E. T. A. Hoffmann and Ludwig Tieck. Hoffmann's children's favorite, for example, *Nußknacker und Mausekönig* [Nutcracker and Mouse King, 1816] is a case in point. There the central character, little Marie, escapes with her nutcracker groom from her unimaginative family into a world of perpetual fantasy. Hauff admired Hoffmann, but his own tales do not show bohemian figures like struggling artists and musicians encountering the supernatural. His protagonists tend to be humble people who do not wrestle with religious or spiritual conflicts. Nor do they slide in and out of phantasmagoric worlds, but rather inhabit a universe with clearly defined boundaries between the real and the magical. In this universe where the supernatural has its role, they must also learn to cope with everyday, material existence and find a place in society. His characters delight in sensuous experiences that actually exist: powerful aromas, tasty food, or the heady pleasures of tobacco and drink. It is easy to identify with the social milieu of these tales – the marketplace, the shoemaker's shop, and, of course, the kitchen. Such material and worldly pleasures held as much appeal for Hauff as did any magical escape into fantasy.

He drew on several sources for his inspiration. In addition to the Grimms' tales, these included the popular *Thousand and One Nights* (cleansed of their erotic content). Contemporary French and German writers provided him with material as well. When he submitted his first *Märchenalmanach* [Fairy Tale Almanac] to an editor in Stuttgart in 1825, he described his intended audience as boys and girls between the ages of twelve and fifteen. He explained that he had conceived the texts in order to present moral principles to this age group without being openly didactic. In so doing, he hit upon a formula that found immediate and lasting favor.

Although Hauff did not develop a theory of the modern fairy tale, he did make his objectives clear in the allegorical prologue to the first collection, *The Caravan*. Here he uses the engaging device of presenting the fictionalized figure of Fairy Tale as a character in a little anecdote. This protago⁄ nist, Fairy Tale, is the daughter of Queen Fantasy, ruler of an enchanted realm of eternal sunshine, who has given the human race gifts to lighten the sadness of toil on earth and, thanks to Fantasy, the human race can endure life's hard⁄ ships. One day, however, Fairy Tale reports to her mother that she has been denied entrance to the world, barred from contact with humans, even shut out of the hearts of chil⁄ dren, who now view her with mistrust. The opinionated hypocrite, Fashion, has spread malignant rumors against Fairy Tale, and border guards patrol the boundary between the land of Fantasy and the human world to prevent her from entering. The queen responds by disguising Fairy Tale as an almanac. In this form, she can cross the border unde⁄ tected and reach an audience of those children who are still innocent of their elders' prejudices. On earth, hostile men armed with sharp pens challenge her. To defend herself, Fairy Tale calls upon her most charming wiles and potent powers of description to explain the innocence of her mis⁄ sion. Conjuring up exotic images of beasts, riders, seas, deserts, forests, and battles, she charms her opponents into sleep, and enters the gate to the earthly world unharmed.

It is easy to discern the meaning of Hauff's little fable: tales of fantasy, which have fallen victim to critics and publishers, are ripe for renewal in the guise of a new medium, the literary almanac. Almanacs were indeed extremely popular in the age of the lending library, which catered to an ever-growing public of readers. This inexpensive medium enabled authors to reach large audiences eager for entertainment.

The two stories illustrated here use an age-old literary structure – the frame story – familiar from such popular collections of tales as *The Thousand and One Nights* or Boccaccio's *Decamaron*. In Hauff's first *Märchenalmanach* the narrator of the first tale is a character in the fictional frame who entertains his listeners – in this case, merchants leading their caravan across the desert – with stories. The stranger from Baghdad, Selim Baruch by name, joins the caravan and suggests to the travelers that they pass the time at the campsites by telling each other tales. Their different personalities are most audible in the narrator's voices that control the beginning and end of each story, though sometimes they interject comments into the plots themselves. The cycle provides an additional thread for the reader to follow, as the narrative frame encompasses the stories and adds extra layers of plot and characters. Once the caravan finally reaches an oasis, it becomes the turn of a jovial young merchant from Nicea to entertain the group. The story he tells is "The Tale of Little Mook."

Hauff continues this frame narrative into the second *Märchenalmanach* where East meets West in curious ways. The main character in the frame story is the wise and generous Ali Banu, Sheik of Alexandria, and a father who mourns his son taken hostage by the Franks. (This story is set during the time of the Crusades when Muslims called all Germans by this name.) Ali Banu has even traveled unsuccessfully to Germany to seek his son. Now he commemorates the abduction once a year by freeing twelve slaves who must each tell a story. There are always many Franks among those released so that Ali Banu may find favor with the prophet and hasten the return of his own son. The first German slave narrates "Dwarf Longnose" for his master's amusement.

These two tales show that Hauff's experience as a tutor prepared him well to write children's stories. He was keenly aware of the expectations of his audience and knew how to entertain both them and their parents. New readers of his stories will notice the absence of terrifying situations, such as violent death or abandonment of children in hostile environments (both common among the Grimms' tales). The *Nursery and Household Tales* often show children oppressed by cruel adults, suffering grief and loss, enduring abandonment, orphanhood, and threats of death in many guises. Of course, these themes are also the primal fears and social tensions of great literature. Hauff, therefore, does not completely banish them, even from his gentler, more modern tales, but he does not dwell on their terrors or let them upstage his lively intrigues.

Children and a child's point of view lie at the center of Hauff's fictions. Both of the tales in this book also abound in reversals of fortune, in which the heroes acquire magical objects that bring them power, only to lose them again. Both youthful protagonists find themselves unwillingly captured and forced to serve sorceresses, but both acquire practical skills during their captivities, and both escape by their wits. They also encounter capricious monarchs and find ways to evade their threats. Some readers have understood this aspect of Hauff's stories as political satire aimed at princely authority, but on the other hand, the figure of the impulsive, repressive monarch is a stock character in *Märchen*. This folk tradition has always served those at the bottom of society, forced to look up at authority figures, by allowing them to depict their superiors unflatteringly and show them ultimately thwarted.

Even more important for Hauff is the theme of the body: both Little Mook and Jacob (in "Dwarf Longnose") are deformed. Mook is born physically misshapen, while Jacob becomes disfigured by magical transformation. These physical traits bring ostracism and test the protagonists' courage. Little Mook uses magic to impose deformity on his tormentors to teach them a moral lesson, while Jacob is punished with deformity in order to learn tolerance and kindness. Both situations unmask the cruelty of society toward those who are different, but in neither tale does Hauff's narrator preach or moralize. Instead, he allows his audience to draw its own conclusions. Magical transfor‑ mations are, of course, the stock in trade of the fantastic tradition, from Homer's *Odyssey* (where Circe changes men into swine) to Kafka's *Metamorphosis*, where a traveling sales‑ man awakens trapped in the body of a beetle. The disfig‑ urement that Jacob suffers in the tale of Dwarf Longnose also prefigures a famous fictional successor, *Pinocchio* (1883), by Carlo Lorenzini (Collodi), where temporary deformity also punishes bad behavior.

Children and adults alike can sense how much Hauff cherishes family stability. This concern is partly a reflection of an age in which an emerging middle class was asserting its taste and values. For both characters, Little Mook as well as Jacob, family relationships (or their absence) are crucial. When the village children understand the story of Mook – a sad, brave, odd‑looking orphan – they ultimately learn tolerance for their neighbor. Before the final reunion with his parents, Jacob in "Dwarf Longnose" is tested by a long separation from them and, later, by their denial. Here Hauff avoids a conventional fairy tale ending, in which Jacob and the sorcerer's daughter would have mar‑ ried to live happily ever after in a distant land. Instead, he rewards Jacob's tribulations by reuniting him with his parents, which suggests that the reconstitution of this family carries more importance than speculation about Jacob's future personal happiness. These are, after all, moral tales rather than fantasies of adult wish fulfillment, so it is sufficient that Jacob regains the harmony and stability of his parental family. By contrast, the end of "Little Mook" strikes a note of resignation. Although the protagonist has the respect of society, he continues to live with his settled prosperity in isolation. In each case Hauff thwarts our expectations. There is no public celebration of the hero's success, as each individual who has been tested in the world is finally left to cope with private concerns. Both leave the world of fantasy behind and return to normalcy with greater wisdom but without any magical charms or amulets. When all is said and done, Hauff's tales domesticate the fantastic. Despite their exotic trappings, his stories bring readers and listeners home to endorse comfort, humane values, and familial affection.

Thomas S. Hansen
Wellesley, Massachusetts

The Tale of
Little Mook

N NICEA, BELOVED CITY
of my birth, there lived a man they called Lit‑
tle Mook. I remember him well, although I
was still very young back then, especially be‑
cause my father once beat me half to death because of him.
You see, Little Mook was already old when I knew him, yet
he was only three or four shoes tall. He was a strange sight,
with his weak little body and enormous head, much larger
than other people's. He lived all alone in a big house where
he cooked for himself. Since he went out only once a month,
people would not have known if he was alive or dead had
it not been for the huge cloud of steam that appeared from
his house every day around noon. You could see him often
from the street in the evenings as he walked up and down
on his roof. From below it looked as if his head were tak‑
ing a stroll all by itself.

My friends and I were mischievous boys who liked to tease and laugh at everyone. For us it was like a holiday when Little Mook went outdoors. We used to gather at his house on the appointed day and wait for him. When the door opened, first the big head, then an even bigger turban emerged. Then out came the rest of his little body covered with a shabby coat, loose trousers, and a wide belt from which a dagger hung – a dagger so long that you couldn't tell if Mook was attached to the dagger or the dagger to Mook. When he walked out looking like this, we filled the air with shrieks of joy. We tossed our caps high and danced around him in a frenzy. Little Mook, however, greeted us with a serious nod of his head and continued to walk slowly down the street, scuffing along in his huge slippers, looser than any I had ever seen. We boys ran behind him shout-ing, "Little Mook, Little Mook!" We even sang a funny rhyme in his honor:

Little Mook, Little Mook!
All month long you stay inside,
Come on out and do not hide.
For a dwarf you may be wise,
But your head is giant size!
Come outdoors and take a look,
Run and catch us, Little Mook!

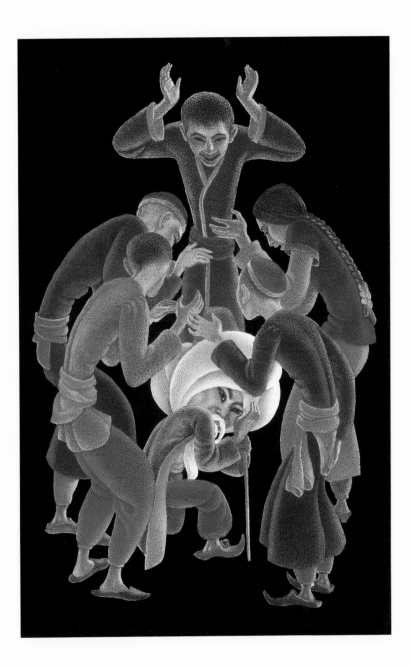

That was how we often had our fun and, I have to confess to my own discredit, I teased him the worst, sometimes tugging at his coat or stepping on his huge slippers to trip him. This all seemed funny to me, but my laughter stopped when I saw Little Mook turn toward my father's house. He went right inside and stayed there for some time. I found a place to hide by the front door and watched Mook come out, accompanied by my father who respectfully extended his hand to the visitor and parted from him at the door, bowing politely several times. I had a bad feeling about this, so I stayed in my hiding place for a long time until hunger forced me out. I feared hunger even more than getting slapped, and so I went to my father hanging my head in shame. "I hear that you've been making fun of good old Mook," he said in a serious voice. "I am going to tell you the story of this fellow and then you certainly won't laugh at him any more. Before and after you'll get the usual." "The usual" consisted of twenty-five whacks, which he counted out all too accurately. So he took his long pipe stem, removed the amber mouthpiece, and worked me over harder than ever. When he had delivered the twenty-five, he ordered me to pay attention while he told the tale of Little Mook.

Little Mook's father, whose name was Mukrah, was a poor but respected man here in Nicea who lived the hermit's life almost as completely as his son does now. But because he was ashamed of his son's small size, he couldn't stand the boy. For this reason, he raised him in ignorance. Up until the age of sixteen Little Mook was a boisterous child, and his father, an earnest man, often scolded him for his silly, boyish ways.

One day the old man suffered a terrible fall and died, leaving Little Mook poor and ignorant. Mook's cold-hearted relatives, to whom the dead man owed more money than he could pay, chased the poor little boy out of the house and told him to go out into the world to seek his fortune. Little Mook answered that he was ready to leave, but asked for his father's clothing, which they gave him. His father had been a big, strong man, so the clothes did not fit. Little Mook started lopping off everything that was too long before he put the clothes on. But he seemed to have forgotten to trim the parts that were too big in the waist, which explains the strange costume he wears to this day. The great turban, wide belt, flapping trousers, blue coat – all of these he inherited from his father. He tucked his father's long silver dagger into his belt, picked up a walking stick, and trudged out through the city gates.

All day he walked, happy because he was setting out to seek his fortune. Whenever he found a pebble that sparkled in the sunshine, he put it in his pocket, believing that it would turn into a beautiful diamond. If he saw the dome of a mosque sparkling like fire in the distance, or a lake shimmering like a mirror, he rushed toward them, thinking he had arrived in a magic land. But oh, the disappointment when those mirages disappeared as he approached them. Soon enough his fatigue and growling stomach reminded him that he was still in the land of mortals. For two days he traveled like this, suffering hunger and hardship, and ready to despair of ever finding his fortune. The fruits of the field were his only food, the hard earth his bed. Then, on the morning of the third day, he climbed a hill and spied a great city where the crescent moon shone on the towers, and colorful flags flew above the roofs, as though waving to him. "Yes, Little Mook will find his fortune there," he said to himself. Despite his weariness, he leapt into the air with joy: "There or nowhere!"

Gathering all his strength, Little Mook made for the city. It looked so near, but his tired little legs almost gave out on him. He had to rest in the shade of a palm tree, and did not reach the city before noon. Finally, he approached the city gate and paused to straighten his coat, tie his turban carefully, tighten his belt, and adjust his dagger. Then he brushed the dust from his shoes, picked up his stick, and marched bravely through the gate. He wandered through the streets, but nowhere did a door open or a voice call out,

"Little Mook, come in! Eat, drink, and rest your little feet!" He was just looking up with longing at a big, beautiful house when a window opened and an old woman shouted out in a sing-song voice:

> Come in, come in,
> Where have you all been?
> I've just set the table,
> So eat what you're able.
> My broth is a treat,
> So, neighbors, come eat!

When the front door opened, Mook saw several dogs and cats go in. He waited a few moments, not knowing whether he too should accept this strange invitation, but once he got his courage up, he decided to follow the animals. He stayed a few steps behind a pair of kittens who knew their way to the kitchen better than he did.

When Mook climbed the steps, who stood before him but the old woman who had poked her head out the window? She eyed him suspiciously and asked what he wanted. "You invited everybody for broth," answered Little Mook, "I came along too, because I'm so hungry." She laughed out loud and said, "Where do you come from, you strange fellow? The whole city knows that I cook only for my precious cats." Little Mook told the old woman how difficult life

had been for him since his father's death and begged her to let him eat with her cats that day. The woman liked the little fellow's honest tale so much that she not only allowed him to be her guest but gave him plenty to eat and drink.

When Little Mook had eaten his fill and recovered his strength, the woman looked at him and said, "Little Mook, why not stay here and work for me? The work is not hard and you will be treated well." Little Mook, who had enjoyed the cats' broth, agreed to become the servant of Madame Ahavzi and carry out an easy but odd task. He had to comb the fur of Madame Ahavzi's six cats every morning and rub them with precious ointments. When Madame Ahavzi went out, he was supposed to look after the cats, give them their dishes of food at mealtimes, and, at night, place them on their silk cushions and cover them with velvet blankets. He also had to keep an eye on some small dogs that lived in the house, but they did not get the same elaborate care as the cats. These Madame Ahavzi treated as her own children. By the way, Little Mook lived just as lonely an existence here as in his father's house. Apart from the old woman, he saw nobody but the cats and dogs.

For a while, things went well for Little Mook. The work was easy and the food plentiful. The old woman seemed pleased with him. But eventually, the cats began to misbehave when the old woman went out. They jumped wildly around the rooms, knocking things over and breaking beautiful objects in their way – until they heard the old woman coming up the stairs. Then they crept up onto their pillows and waved their tails gently to and fro as though nothing had happened. Madame Ahavzi grew furious when she saw such destruction, and she immediately blamed Little Mook. However much he asserted his innocence, she refused to trust her servant, preferring to trust the cats who just lay there looking blameless.

Little Mook was very sad that he had not found his fortune there, and decided to leave Madame Ahavzi's household. But because his first journey into the world had taught him how bad life is without any money, he decided to get his hands on the salary Madame Ahavzi had promised but never paid. There was a room in the house that she always kept closed, and he had never entered it. He had often heard the old woman poking around behind the door, and for his life would have loved to know what she had hidden in it. Now that his mind was on money, it occurred to him that Madame Ahavzi might keep her treasure locked up in this room.

One morning, when Madame Ahavzi had gone out, one of her little dogs scampered up to Mook. The old woman had always treated this dog poorly, but it was a favorite of Mook's. Now it began to tug at Mook's trouser leg as though asking him to follow. Mook liked to play with the dogs, so he followed happily. But imagine what this dog was up to: it led him straight through Madame Ahavzi's bedroom to a little door in the wall that Mook had never seen before. The door was half open. The dog went through the doorway and Mook followed. He was overcome with joy when he found himself in the locked chamber that had always been the object of his curiosity. He looked around for money, but found only old clothes and vessels of strange and marvelous form. One that caught his attention was made of crystal and had beautiful figures etched on it. He picked it up and turned it to examine it from all sides, when – oh, horror! – its lid, which he had not noticed, fell to the floor and shattered into a thousand pieces.

For the longest time Little Mook stood there petrified with fear. Now his fate was sealed: he had no choice but to flee before the old woman killed him. With his journey decided, he cast another glance around the room to see if he could use any of Madame Ahavzi's possessions on the long march ahead. His eye fell upon a pair of enormous slippers. They were not particularly beautiful, but their huge size appealed to him, for with them on his feet people would see that he had clearly outgrown children's shoes. So he took off his little old slippers and stepped into the big new ones. In the corner, there stood a little walking stick with a carved lion's head. Thinking that there was no need to let that stay idly behind, Mook grabbed it as he rushed from the room. Then he went quickly to his own room, put on his coat and his father's turban, stuck the dagger in his belt, and ran as fast his feet could carry him from the house, straight out of the city.

Beyond the city walls, fear of the old woman drove him on until weariness almost made him fall over. He had never gone so fast in his life, but still, he kept running. It seemed as though an invisible force kept pulling him onward! He finally noticed that this had something to do with the slip-pers. They kept darting forward, dragging him with them. He tried everything he could to stand still but nothing worked. Then he cried out in desperation, "Oh, stop, stop!" His words brought the slippers to a halt and Mook fell to the ground, exhausted.

His new slippers delighted him. He had actually gotten some payment for his services that could help him seek his fortune in the world. Despite his joy, he fell asleep, for his body, which had to carry such a large head, could not en-dure very much. In his dreams the little dog that had helped him get the slippers appeared, and spoke. It said: "My dear Mook, you don't yet understand how to use your new slip-pers. Just think, when you spin on your heel three times you can fly wherever you wish. And with the walking stick you can find treasure: it will strike the earth three times where gold is buried and twice for silver." That was Little Mook's marvelous dream.

When he awoke, he thought about the dream and decided to try an experiment. He put on the slippers, lifted one foot in the air and began to turn on his heel. If you have ever tried to perform such a feat three times in a row in a pair of slippers several sizes too large for you, you won't be surprised that Little Mook couldn't do it either at first, especially considering how his heavy head bobbed from side to side.

The poor little fellow fell on his nose a few times, but he kept trying until it finally worked. He spun on his heel like a wheel, wished himself in the next big city – and the slippers paddled him up into the sky and whooshed him through the clouds. Before Little Mook realized what was happening, he found himself in a large market square. Crowds of people hurried back and forth among booths. He walked among the people but soon found it wiser to go off into a quieter street. For sometimes in the crowded market, people almost tripped him by stepping on his slippers, or his big dagger would poke people, which made them slap him – something he preferred to avoid.

Little Mook now thought seriously about earning money. Of course, he had his staff, which could show him buried treasure. But where do you begin looking for places where

gold and silver could be buried? It occurred to him that he could charge people money just to look at him, but he was much too proud for that. Remembering at last the speed of his feet, he realized that his slippers could save him, so he decided to find work as a messenger. Since he dared to hope that the king of the city would pay his servants the highest wages, he asked the way to the palace. At the palace gate, he found a guard who asked him his business. When the guard heard that Little Mook was looking for a job, he sent him to the slave master. Mook asked this fellow for a job as a royal messenger, but the slave master looked him up and down and said, "How do you expect to become a royal messenger with those tiny little feet? Get out of here! It's not my job to joke around with every fool in town." Little Mook assured him, however, that he was serious, and that he would let a foot race against the fastest messenger decide the outcome. The slave master, who thought this idea amusing, told him to prepare for a race that very evening. In the meantime, he showed him to the kitchen, where he could eat and drink his fill. While Mook ate, the slave master went right to the king to report on Little Mook and his proposition.

The king, a jolly fellow, was amused that his slave master was having a joke with Little Mook, so he ordered that the race be held before the entire court on a large field behind the palace. He warned the slave master to take good care of the dwarf, then told all the princes and princesses about the show they were going to enjoy that evening. They passed this news along to their attendants, so that by evening, everybody was in a state of high expectation. At the appointed time, all who could walk assembled at the field, where benches had been set up for them to watch the boastful dwarf run the foot race.

When the king and all his royal children had taken their seats, Little Mook entered the field and bowed gracefully to the whole court. The sight of Mook made everyone cheer with joy, for nobody had ever seen anything like him. The little body with its great head, the little coat and flowing trousers, the long blade in the wide belt, the tiny feet in the huge slippers – it was all so funny, who could help laughing? Little Mook was not insulted by this amusement. He stood there proudly, leaning on his walking stick, waiting for his opponent to enter. The slave master had, of course, chosen the fastest runner of all the royal messengers, who now came out and stood beside Mook to wait for the starting signal. Princess Amarza waved her veil and, like two arrows, the runners shot across the field toward the goal.

Mook's opponent had a clear advantage from the start, but Mook used his magic to catch up with him. There he was, standing at the goal when the man finally arrived panting. Amazement gripped the onlookers who sat in stunned silence. Finally, when the king began to clap, the crowd rejoiced, shouting, "Hurrah for Little Mook, the winner of the race!"

When Mook was brought before the king, he bowed low and said: "Great and mighty king, today I have shown you only a tiny sample of my powers. Grant me, I beg you, a place among your messengers." But the king said, "No, I shall make you my Personal Royal Runner so that I shall always have you near me, my dear Mook. As a reward, you will receive one hundred gold pieces a year and dine at the same table as my most important servants."

With this, Mook thought he had at last found the fortune he had sought for so long, and his heart overflowed with happiness. He enjoyed the special favor of the king, who used him to deliver his most secret messages, which he did to perfection and with baffling speed.

The other court servants, however, were not at all happy with Little Mook. They thought they had lost favor with the king, and that a dwarf, whose only talent was running fast, was overshadowing their talents. So they began to plot against him, but their evil plans failed thanks to the great trust the king placed in his Personal Royal Runner, a title no other servant of the king's had ever attained.

Mook knew that feelings against him were growing. But rather than plot revenge – his heart was too pure for that – he looked for ways to turn his enemies into friends. He thought of his magic walking stick, which he had not used yet, for he hoped that the king's servants would like him more if he could find buried treasure. It had frequently come to his ears that the father of the present king had buried much of his treasure when the kingdom was under siege. It was also said that he had died before he could tell his son about this secret. From that point on Mook always carried his staff with him in the hope that he would pass the place where the old king's gold was buried. One evening, chance brought him to a distant corner of the palace garden where he seldom visited. Suddenly his stick began to twitch. Three times it struck the ground! He knew what that meant and drew his dagger to mark the surrounding trees before sneaking back into the palace to fetch a shovel. He waited at the spot until very late at night before beginning his task.

Digging for buried treasure by himself was more work than Mook ever imagined. Because his arms were weak and his shovel long and heavy, he dug for over two hours before getting down even two feet. Finally, he struck something hard that sounded like metal. Digging even harder, he soon uncovered a big, iron lid. He climbed down into the hole to see what the lid covered and found a great pot filled with gold coins. He did not have enough strength to lift the pot, so he filled his trousers and belt with as much gold as he could carry. He even filled his coat, which he slung over his shoulder. The gold weighed him down so heavily that, without his magic slippers, he never would have been able to move from the spot at all. Still, he got to his room unnoticed and hid his gold under the pillows on his sofa.

Once he realized just how much gold he had, Little Mook thought he could finally change things at the court and turn his many rivals into allies. But alas, you can see this was just more proof that good Little Mook had no idea about the ways of the world. Otherwise, he would have known that you cannot buy friends with gold. Oh, if only he had spun around on his magic slippers right there and disappeared like a puff of smoke with his coat full of gold!

This gold, which Little Mook now began to give away at court with both hands, aroused nothing but envy in the other servants. Ahuli, the cook, said, "He must be a counterfeiter!" Achmet, the slave master, said, "He must have swindled the king out of this money!" Archaz, the Royal Treasurer (Mook's bitterest enemy who himself, now and then, dipped into the treasury), said, "He stole it!"

To present their case against Mook, the king's First Chamberlain Korchuz went before his master with gloomy, downcast eyes. He looked so unhappy that the king asked him what was wrong. The chamberlain answered, "I am sad because I have obviously lost Your Majesty's favor." "What

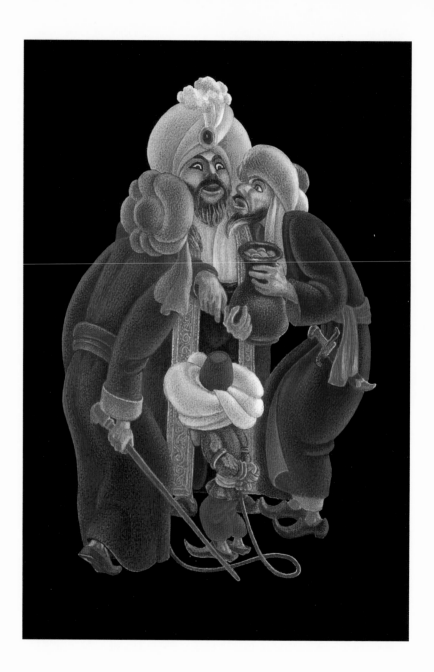

can you possibly be imagining, friend Korchuz?" the king replied. "Since when has the sun of my favor stopped shining over you?" The First Chamberlain answered that His Majesty seemed to be heaping gold upon his Personal Royal Runner, Mook, while his other faithful servants received nothing.

Shocked at this news, the king asked for the whole story about Little Mook and the gold. This made it easy for the conspirators to suggest that Mook had stolen the money from the treasury. The Royal Treasurer, who – to put it politely – kept rather sketchy accounts of his master's money, loved this turn of events. The king ordered that Mook be followed at every step from then on and, if possible, caught redhanded. So it happened that late one night, Mook's reserves ran out and he took his shovel and sneaked out to the palace garden to replenish his gold from the pot of buried treasure. At this point, the guards (led by the cook and the Royal Treasurer) grabbed him, tied him up, and hauled him before the king.

His Majesty, annoyed at having his sleep disturbed, received his poor Personal Royal Runner harshly and started questioning him. The pot of gold had been dug up and placed at the king's feet beside the shovel and Mook's coat full of coins. The Royal Treasurer swore that he had surprised Mook just as he was burying the pot, so the king began by asking the accused if this were true, and where the gold had come from. Little Mook spoke with all the force of his innocence, saying that he had found the pot in the garden and was not burying it, but digging it up!

Everyone had a good laugh at this defense. The king, enraged at what he took to be Mook's insolence, shouted, "What? You miserable little man! You dare to lie to your king as well as rob him? Royal Treasurer Archaz! I demand to know: is this the same amount of money that is missing from my treasury?" The treasurer said yes, he was certain of it. In fact, even more was missing, and he would swear that this was the stolen money.

So the king then ordered Mook to be led in chains to the tower. The Royal Treasurer took the money, supposedly to replace it in the king's coffers, but instead he went straight home and, thrilled with this whole affair, began to count the shining gold pieces. But there was something this villain did not know: at the bottom of the pot of gold there lay a note with these words:

The enemy has overrun my land, so I am burying part of my treasure here. The royal curse lies upon whoever finds this and does not return it to my son immediately.

– King Saadi

In the dungeon all this while, Little Mook had begun to

lose all hope, for he knew the penalty for stealing from the king was death. Still, he did not want to tell the king the secret of the magic walking stick, because he knew that the stick and his precious slippers would both be stolen from him. By now the slippers were not much help anyway. Chained to the wall, Mook had no way to spin on his heel. The next day, however, when he heard he was to be executed for theft, he decided it was better to live without his walking stick than to die with it. And so he requested a private audience in order to reveal his secret to the king.

The king did not believe a word Mook said, but when Mook promised to prove it in return for his life, the king relented. He ordered Little Mook to demonstrate the powers of the walking stick by finding some gold pieces he had buried in the ground while Mook was not watching. Mook found these with no trouble as soon as the stick struck the earth three times. Realizing that his treasurer had deceived him, the king sent the man a silken cord to strangle himself with, as is the custom in the Orient.

To Little Mook he said, "I have promised you your life, but it seems to me that you have more secrets than just this magic staff. For that you will spend your life in prison until I know how you run so fast." Little Mook's one night in the tower had satisfied any curiosity he might have had about life behind bars, so he admitted the slippers were magical too, but he did not tell the king the secret about turning three times on one's heel! When the king stepped into the slippers to test them, he ran around furiously in the garden. He wanted to stop, but the slippers refused to stand still. Unable to resist this tiny gesture of revenge, Little Mook let the king run until he fell over in a dead faint.

When the king had recovered, he was so furious with Little Mook that he said, "I promised you your freedom and your life, but if you do not leave my land within twelve hours, I'll string you up! The slippers and the walking stick will stay right here in my treasury."

So Little Mook left the king's land as poor as ever, cursing the foolishness that had made him think he could be an important figure at court. Fortunately, the country he was forced to leave was not large. He was able to reach the border in just eight hours, although without his precious slippers the walk was very arduous.

Once he had crossed the border, he left the road and headed for the woods to seek the most isolated place to live, for he was sick of all human company. There, in the dense forest, he came upon a spot he liked. A clear stream bordered by tall, shady fig trees and soft grasses made an inviting sight. Here he flung himself down on the ground where he decided to stop eating and just wait for death. He fell asleep thinking about death, but when he awoke, hunger pangs

convinced him that starvation was a serious matter, and he looked around for something to eat. Mouth-watering ripe figs hung from the trees, so he climbed up and enjoyed some of this fruit. Then he quenched his thirst at the stream. What a shock he had when he saw his reflection in the water! Was that really his head with those oversized ears and long thick nose? Stunned, he grabbed at his ears. It was true, they were as long as your arm.

"I deserve donkey's ears," he cried. "I trampled on my own fortune like an ass!" He wandered under the trees like this until he felt hungry again. When there was nothing else to eat, he had to climb up for more figs. After eating the second portion of figs, he felt that his ears suddenly had more room underneath his big turban. So he ran back to the stream to check his reflection and it was true: his ears were their former size and his long, unsightly nose had disappeared. He also realized how this had happened: the first fig tree had produced the long nose and the big ears, while the second one had removed them. Mook realized with joy that his good luck had handed him another means to find his fortune. So he picked from each tree as many figs as he could carry and returned to the land he had left so recently. Along the way he stopped to disguise himself in different clothes before continuing on to the capital where the king lived.

It happened to be the time of year when ripe fruit was

out of season. Little Mook sat down near the palace gate, for he knew from past experience that merchants often met the royal cook there to sell him delicacies for the king's table. Soon enough, the cook came across the courtyard and began to inspect the morning's offerings. When he noticed Mook's basket, he said, "Aha, ripe figs, a rare morsel that should please His Majesty! What will you take for the whole basket?" Little Mook agreed to a moderate price and they struck a deal. A slave carried the figs away while Mook made tracks in the other direction for fear they would come after the seller and punish him once the expected catastrophe had occurred.

The king happened to be in a jolly mood at the table that day. He lavished praise on the cook's fine cuisine and the care with which he had chosen and prepared these rare dishes. The cook knew that the biggest treat – ripe figs out of season – was yet to come. He smiled and just said things like, "All's well that ends well," or "The best is for last." This made the princesses very curious about what he might bring next. When the lovely, tempting figs were served, all the noble diners let out a chorus of "Ahs!"

"How ripe and delicious those look! My cook has outdone himself this time and deserves our special favor!" Saying this, the king, who tended to be a bit stingy with such delicacies, divided the figs himself among those at the table. He gave the princes and princesses two each, and one each to the court ladies, the viziers, and the nobles. Then he set all the rest before himself and began to devour them.

"Dear God, father!" cried out Princess Amarza sud⁄denly. "How odd you look!" Everyone looked at the king in astonishment. Huge ears flopped down from his head and a long nose drooped down to his chin! When they looked at each other, they saw to their horror that they were all marked with the same bizarre features.

Imagine the panic! They sent for all the doctors in the city and these worthies came in droves to prescribe pills and tinctures. Still, the floppy ears and long noses remained. The doctors even operated on one of the princes, but the ears grew back.

Mook, who was in hiding, had heard about everything and realized it was time to act. He used the money he had been paid for the figs to buy new clothes so he could now dress as a scholar. A long beard of goat hair completed his disguise. Carrying a little sack of figs, he wandered over to the royal palace and offered his help as a traveling physi⁄cian. At first people were skeptical, but when Mook gave one of the princes a fig that changed his ears and nose back to their old shape, everybody wanted to be cured by this foreign doctor. The king took him silently by the hand and led him into his chamber. There he opened the door

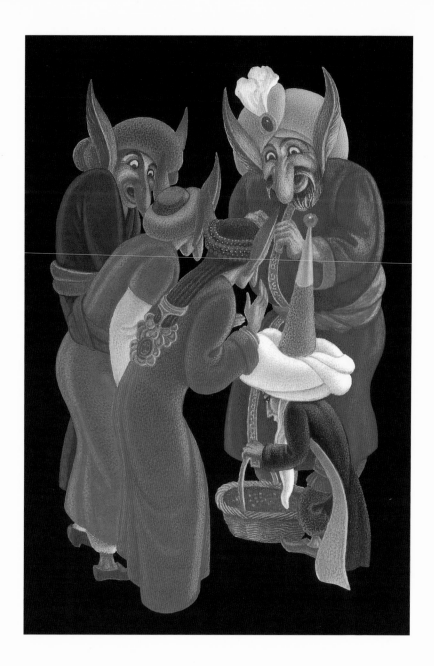

to his treasury and beckoned Mook to follow. "Here are all my riches, choose whatever you desire and it shall be yours, if you can cure me of this awful disfigurement."

His words were sweet music to Little Mook's ears. For one thing, as soon as he had entered the treasury he noticed his magic slippers on the floor. Beside them lay his walking stick. He walked around in the room, as if to marvel at all the king's treasure. When he came to the slippers, he slid into them like lightning, grabbed his walking stick, tore off his false beard, and confronted the king with the familiar face of the Little Mook he had banished. "Faithless king," he said, "because you rewarded loyal service with ingratitude, consider this deformity the punishment you deserve. I leave you your big, floppy ears as a daily reminder of Little Mook." Saying this, Mook spun on his heel, wished himself far away, and escaped before the king could call for help.

Since that time, Little Mook has lived here in splendor, but his life is lonely, for he has turned his back on people. Experience has made him wise. Despite his strange appearance, he deserves your respect more than your scorn.

That was the end of my father's tale. I assured him that I regretted my heartless behavior toward the good little man, and my father gave the second half of the punishment he had promised. I told my comrades the marvelous tale of Little Mook, and we all grew so fond of him that nobody ever

teased him again. Instead, we honored him as long as he lived
and every month when he came out of his lonely house,
we bowed as low to him when he passed
as we would to any sultan.

♦   ♦
♦

Dwarf Longnose

NYONE WHO BELIEVES
that fairies and sorcerers existed only when
Harun Al-Raschid ruled Baghdad – or who
doubts what storytellers in the marketplace
say about the tricks of genies and their princes – is wrong.
Magical beings exist today. In fact, it was not so long ago
that I myself witnessed the workings of just such beings.
Let me tell you about it.

Many years ago in an important city in Germany, my
dear homeland, there lived a plain, honest shoemaker and
his wife. By day he sat in a little shop on the street corner
mending shoes and slippers and taking orders for new
ones from customers. To make these, he first had to buy the
leather, for he was too poor to keep raw materials in stock.
His wife sold fruit and vegetables, which she grew in a small

garden by their gate. Her customers were loyal, for she always looked clean and tidy, and so did the vegetables she sold.

This little couple had a fine son who was handsome and well built. He was a tall boy for a lad of twelve, and went to the market to sit with his mother. He often delivered fruit for the housewives and cooks who bought from the shoe-maker's wife. When he did so, he rarely returned without a pretty flower, a coin, or a piece of cake, for the cooks' mis-tresses enjoyed the sight of a good-looking boy and rewarded him generously.

One day, the shoemaker's wife was sitting as usual in the marketplace. She had her baskets of cabbage and other veg-etables, herbs and seeds, and a small basket of early-ripened pears, apples, and apricots in front of her. Young Jacob, as the boy was called, sat beside her and hawked their wares in a clear voice: "Over here, good sirs, come see the beautiful cabbage, the fragrant herbs. Early pears, good women, early apples and apricots! Who will buy? My mother's prices are the best!"

That day an old woman came walking across the market square. She looked threadbare and ragged and her narrow, little face was wrinkled with age. She had red eyes and a sharp, crooked nose that curved down toward her chin. She walked with a long stick, yet it was hard to say just how she made any progress, for her gait was a tottering limp and shuffle. She almost seemed to have wheels on her feet that could trip her right onto the cobblestones at any moment. The shoemaker's wife, who had come to this marketplace every day for sixteen years, paid close attention to this old woman, for she had never seen such a strange figure before. She was understandably frightened when the old woman limped up to her and stopped in front of her baskets.

"Are you Hanne, the vegetable seller?" the old woman asked. Her voice was creaky and unpleasant and her head constantly wagged from side to side.

"I am," the shoemaker's wife answered. "What would you like?"

"Let me see, let me see! Let's see if you have any seasonings I can use," the old woman said, bending over the baskets. She stuck her ugly, dark brown hands deep into the herbs that were displayed so attractively. One after the other, she pulled out each plant with her spidery fingers, held it up to her long nose, and sniffed it. The shoemaker's wife's heart nearly stopped as she watched the old woman treat her rare herbs that way. Still, she did not dare say anything. After all, the customer is always right. What is more, the old crone really frightened her. When the woman had finished pawing through the basket, she murmured, "Bad stuff, poor herbs, nothing at all I want. Better fifty years ago. Bad stuff, bad stuff!"

These words upset young Jacob. "Just a minute, old hag," he muttered, "First you rummage through our lovely herbs with your horrible, brown fingers. Then you crush them and put them up to your long nose so nobody who saw you would ever want to buy them. And on top of that, you say our wares are bad stuff! Don't you know that the duke's cook buys from us?"

The old woman squinted at the brave boy, let out a hideous laugh, and croaked, "So, child, you like my nose, my beautiful long nose? Then you shall have one too – right in the middle of your face and down to your chin." As she spoke, she lurched over to the basket of cabbages, picked up two prize heads and pressed them together until they squeaked. Then she threw them back into the basket muttering, "Bad stuff, bad stuff!"

"Stop wagging your ugly head like that," the boy called out, sounding braver than he felt. "Your neck is as thin as a cabbage stalk and might break. If your head fell into our basket, nobody would ever buy from us again!"

"So you don't like thin necks?" laughed the old woman. "Then you won't have one. Your head will grow right from your shoulders so you won't have to worry about it falling off your little body."

"Stop talking that nonsense to the boy," the shoemaker's wife finally said, for she was angry at all this squeezing, inspecting, and smelling of her wares. "If you want something, hurry up and buy. You're driving my other customers away."

"As you wish," cried the old woman with an evil look. "I'll take these six heads of cabbage. But because I have to walk with a stick and can't carry anything, you must let your son deliver them for me. I'll pay him for it."

The lad did not want to go with the old woman. He was so afraid of the hideous crone that he began to cry. But his mother said it would be a sin to burden the weak old woman with anything as heavy as the cabbages. Sobbing, he did as he was told. Tying up the basket of cabbages in a cloth, he followed the old woman across the market square.

She did not move very quickly, so it took them three quarters of an hour to reach a distant part of the city where she stopped in front of a shabby, old house. She took a rusty key from her pocket and deftly inserted it into a small hole in the door. The door sprang open with a loud bang.

When Jacob entered, an amazing sight met his eyes. Inside, the house was richly decorated, with marble walls and ceilings. The furnishings were of pure ebony, inlaid with gold and polished stones. And the floor was made of glass so slippery that the boy skidded and fell several times. The old woman pulled a silver whistle from her pocket and played a tune that echoed through the whole house. Right away, a whole troop of guinea pigs came up the stairs. Jacob thought it strange that they walked on their hind legs and wore nutshells on their paws, like shoes. What's more, they were dressed in human clothes and wore hats of the latest fashion.

"Where are my slippers, you wretched rabble?" the old woman shrieked and swiped at them with her stick so they leapt in the air, howling in fear. "Do I have to stand here all day?"

They ran upstairs and returned with a pair of coconut shells lined with leather, which the old woman put on. All her limping and slipping vanished as she threw her staff away and glided swiftly over the glass floor, pulling Jacob by the hand. She finally stopped at a room filled with all sorts of utensils, very much like a kitchen, although the tables were mahogany and there were sofas decked in rich carpets, which seemed more suited to an elegant chamber than a kitchen.

"Sit down, my boy," the old woman said in a friendly voice. She pushed him into a corner of a sofa and shoved a table close against him so he couldn't move. "Sit down and rest. You have had a lot to carry. Human heads are not so light, not so light."

"What do you mean, human heads?" the boy cried. "I carried heads of cabbage! You bought them from my mother."

"Ah, you're wrong there," the old woman laughed. She took the lid off of the basket and pulled a severed human head out by the hair. The boy nearly fainted from terror, for he had no idea how this could have happened. Thinking of his mother, he felt terrified. What if someone found out about these human heads and blamed her for it?

"I want to pay you for your trouble because you have such good manners," the old woman murmured. "Be patient a moment and I'll feed you a soup that you'll remember for the rest of your life." So saying, she blew her whistle again. First, there appeared the guinea pigs, in kitchen aprons with wooden spoons and carving knives in their belts. Then came squirrels, who also walked on their hind legs and wore flow-ing Turkish trousers and green velvet caps. These creatures seemed to be her kitchen boys, for they scampered up the walls and brought down pans and bowls, eggs and butter, and seasonings and flour, which they carried to the hearth. There the old woman raced around on her coconut shell slippers and the boy saw that she was determined to cook him something elaborate. The fire now crackled, and the pan soon simmered and smoked away, filling the room with pleasant smells. The old woman ran back and forth with the squirrels and guinea pigs behind her. Whenever she passed the hearth, she bent over to poke her long nose into the pot. Its contents finally started to hiss and bubble until foam poured over the top into the fire. She removed the pot from the heat and poured a bit of broth into a silver bowl, which she set before Jacob.

"Well, there you are, my boy," she murmured. "Eat this soup and you'll have everything that you liked so much about me. You'll also be a talented cook, so at least you'll have something. But the special herb, no, you'll never find that. Why didn't your mother have it in her basket?"

The boy barely understood a word of what she said, but he paid close attention to the soup, which tasted so good. His mother had cooked him many a tasty meal, but never anything as good as this. An aroma of fine spices and seasonings rose from the soup, which was both sweet and sour. As he drank the last drop of the precious liquid, the guinea pigs lit Arabian incense, which filled the room with clouds of blue smoke. These grew thicker and thicker as they settled heavily in the room, making the boy very sleepy. Even though he told himself that he must return to his mother as soon as he gathered his strength, his eyes kept closing. Soon he was fast asleep on the old woman's sofa.

Here strange dreams visited him. It was as if the old woman were taking off his clothes and dressing him in a squirrel's skin. Suddenly, he was a member of the troops of squirrels and guinea pigs and could leap and climb just like them. They all seemed to be good, courteous creatures who served the old woman in her house. At first, he was put to work as a humble shoe cleaner, who polished the old woman's coconut shells with oil until they shone. Because he was used to such chores in his father's house, this task was easy. After about a year in his dream, he rose to a more elegant job. With some of the other squirrels, he caught motes of dust from sunbeams and, when they had gathered enough, rubbed these through a sieve made of the finest hair. The old woman, who was toothless and could not chew well, thought this sunbeam dust the finest flour in the world, and had all her bread made from these particles.

After another year, he advanced to working with the squirrel servants who collected drinking water for the old woman. You mustn't think they just dug a well or placed a rainwater barrel in the courtyard to get this water. The old woman demanded something much finer than that. The squirrels, and Jacob along with them, had to ladle fresh dew from the roses with hazelnut shells, for this was all the old woman would drink. And because she was forever thirsty, her water carriers were always hard at work.

After another year passed, Jacob got another promotion. He joined the house staff as a floor cleaner. Remember, these were glass floors that showed the slightest smudge, so this was no small task. The floor cleaners had to scrub every inch of glass and then slide on it with polishing clothes tied

to their feet. In the fourth year, however, Jacob finally advanced to the kitchen – an honorable position that one could earn only after years of trying. Jacob served there first as a kitchen boy, but he worked his way up to head pastry chef and developed such skill in everything related to cooking that he sometimes even surprised himself. The most difficult things came easily: pies made of two hundred different ingredients, herbal soups made of all the seasonings of the world – he quickly learned to make all sorts of complicated dishes.

Thus it happened that one day when he had been in the service of the old woman for seven years, she took off her coconut shoes, picked up her walking stick, and announced she was going out. She ordered Jacob to pluck her a chicken, prepare it with an herbal stuffing, and roast it to a golden brown before she returned. All this he did with expert technique. He wrung the chicken's neck, plunged it into hot water, plucked the feathers, scraped the skin smooth, and gutted it. Then he set about gathering the herbs to make a stuffing. In the herb pantry, a little wall cupboard that he had not seen before caught his eye. The door was ajar, and he was curious to see its contents. Inside he found many small baskets that smelled wonderful. He opened one and found tiny herbs of a peculiar shape and color. Its stems and leaves were blue-green; its blossoms were fiery red with

yellow borders. As he contemplated these plants, he realized that they gave off the same aroma as the soup the old
woman had given him so many years ago. The smell was so
powerful that he began to sneeze – more and more force-
fully – until he awakened.

   He lay there on the old woman's sofa quite bewildered.
"No, it's not possible for a dream to seem so real!" he said
to himself. "I could have sworn that I was a squirrel, a
comrade of guinea pigs and other little, furry creatures,
and that I rose to become a great chef. How my mother will
laugh when I tell her this. But won't she scold me for falling
asleep in a strange house when I should be helping her on
market day?"

   With these thoughts he made a huge effort and got up.
His arms and legs were stiff from his nap, and he could
hardly move his head. He had to laugh at himself for being
so drowsy that he kept bumping into walls or pieces of
furniture with his nose. When he turned around quickly,
he crashed against a doorjamb. The squirrels and guinea
pigs ran around him whimpering as if they wanted to come
along. At the doorstep of the house he beckoned them to
follow, for they were cute little animals. But they turned
around on their little nutshell shoes and ran back inside.
Outside, he heard them wailing in the distance.

   The old woman had led him to such a distant part of

the city that he could barely find his way home through the narrow streets. What's more, he imagined that there must have been a dwarf somewhere near him in the crowds, because he heard people yelling, "Look at the ugly dwarf! Where's he from? Look how his head grows right from his shoulders, and look at those ugly, brown hands." At any other time he would have run along with the crowd, for he liked seeing strange sights like giants, dwarves, or travelers in foreign costume. But as it was, he was in a hurry to get back to his mother.

By the time he reached the marketplace, he was in a state of panic. His mother was still sitting there and her fruit baskets were full, so he couldn't have slept very long. But from a distance he could see that she was very sad, for she didn't call the passers-by to come and see her wares, but sat silent, with her chin on her hand. The closer he got, the paler she looked. Not knowing what to do, he finally took heart. Putting a hand on her arm, he said, "Mother, what is wrong? Are you angry with me?"

When his mother turned toward him, she recoiled and shrieked, "What do want, ugly dwarf? Get out of here! Don't mock me like that!"

"But mother, what's wrong?" Jacob asked, just as shocked as she was. "I can see you are not well, but why would you chase your son away?"

"I told you, go away," his mother shouted. "You won't get any money from me with your tricks, you ugly monster."

"By God, she's gone mad," the boy said to himself. "How will I ever get her home now?" Out loud he said, "Dear Mother, be reasonable. Look at me. I am your son, Jacob."

"That's it. This joke has gone too far," Hanne called out to the woman beside her. "Look at this disgusting dwarf standing here and driving away my customers. He dares to mock my misfortune. He even says he's my lovely son Jacob. What nerve!"

The other market women stood up and joined the scolding – market women, in case you didn't know, are good at this. They berated him for taking advantage of Hanne's misfortune, a woman whose beautiful boy had been stolen seven years ago. They threatened to scratch him to pieces if he didn't disappear at once.

Poor Jacob did not know what to make of all this. Hadn't he gone to market this morning with his mother as usual? Hadn't he helped her set up the stall to display their fruits and vegetables? Hadn't he delivered a basket to the house of the old woman who had made him soup? Hadn't he just taken a nap and then come right back? What were these market women saying about seven years? Why were they calling him a hideous dwarf? What had happened to him?

When he realized that his mother really wanted nothing more to do with him, tears came to his eyes and he sadly made his way down the street to the shop where his father mended shoes. "I'll see if he recognizes me. I'll sit by the door and speak with him." When he arrived at the cobbler's shop, he looked inside, but the shoemaker was too busy to look up from his work. At one point, however, he did glance toward the door. Then he dropped his shoes, twine, and awl onto the floor and cried out, "For God's sake, what is that?"

"Good evening, Master," said the boy as he entered the shop. "How are you?"

"Not well, not well, little fellow," answered Jacob's father looking confused, for he did not seem to recognize the boy either. "My business isn't going well. I am alone here and getting old and can't afford an apprentice."

"But don't you have a son you can teach your craft?" the boy asked.

"I had one. His name was Jacob. By now he must be a tall, clever lad of nineteen who could be my right hand these days. Ha, that would be a life! When he was only twelve he was bright and eager and really understood this business – a handsome lad who attracted so many customers that soon I wasn't just mending old shoes any more but mak⁄ing brand new ones." He sighed, "Oh well, that's the way of the world!"

"Where is your son?" Jacob asked his father, his voice shaking.

"Only the good Lord knows," he answered. "Seven years ago – that's how long it is now – he was stolen from us in the marketplace."

"Seven years ago!" Jacob was astonished.

"Yes, little sir, seven years ago. It seems like yesterday that my wife came home sobbing and frantic. Our boy had been missing all day. She looked everywhere and couldn't find him. I was always afraid this might happen. Jacob was so beautiful. We were so proud of him. We loved it when people praised him, so we let him deliver goods to wealthy households. That was all right; he always got a good tip. But I said, 'Be careful, the city is big and filled with a lot of bad types.' I told my wife to take care of Jacob. And then it happened just as I feared. An ugly old woman came to the market, haggled over some fruit and vegetables, and finally bought more than she could carry. My wife, who is soft-hearted, let our son carry her market basket for her – and that was the last we saw of him."

"And it's been seven years, you say?"

"Seven years this spring. We sent out the town crier. We went from house to house ourselves and asked. People who had known and loved our handsome boy helped us search – but it was no use. Nobody even seemed to know the woman who had bought the vegetables. But there was an ancient woman, at least ninety years old, who said that it could have been the evil herb sorceress who comes to town every fifty years looking for plants."

Jacob's father told his story as he hammered at his shoes and pulled the twine through the leather with both fists. Jacob realized what had happened to him. He had not been dreaming, but had really served the sorceress for seven years as a squirrel. His heart was nearly breaking from anger and misery. The old woman had stolen seven years of his youth, and what had he gotten in return? Shining coconut slippers, tied with rags to clean a huge glass floor? All the kitchen secrets of the guinea pigs? He stood there a good while and thought about his fate. Then his father asked him, "Does the young gentleman desire any of my handi-work? A pair of new slippers perhaps, or," he added with a smile, "a nice leather case for your nose?"

"What's wrong with my nose?" asked Jacob. "Why should I need a case for it?"

"Well," replied the cobbler, "to each his own. But I must say, if I had that horrible nose, I'd have a case made for it out of shiny pink leather. Look, I have a nice piece right here. Of course, it will take at least a yard, but then you'd be protected. As it is, I'll bet you hit every door and wagon that you try to avoid."

Jacob felt all along the length of his nose. It was thick and least two hands long! So the old woman had also changed the way he looked! That was why his mother had not known him and why people called him an ugly dwarf. "Master," he said to the shoemaker, half in tears, "Do you happen to have a mirror?"

"Young sir," his father answered sternly, "with your looks there is no cause to be vain. If you are used to preening in the mirror, I would break that ridiculous habit, if I were you."

"Please let me look in a mirror," Jacob cried. "I promise you, it is not out of vanity!"

"Forget it, I have no such thing. My wife has one, but I don't know where she keeps it. If you really need to see a mirror, go down the street to Urban the barber. He has one twice as big as your head. Look into that, and in the meantime, good day to you."

With these words his father shoved him gently out of his shop, closed the door, and sat back down to work. Dejected, Jacob went down the street to Urban the barber, whom he knew from earlier times. "Good morning, Urban," he said to him, "I have come to ask you a favor. Would you kindly let me look into your mirror?"

"With pleasure. There it stands," said the barber with a laugh. His customers, who were there to get their beards shaved, had a good laugh too. "You're a handsome devil, you are – tall and slender, with a neck like a swan and hands like a queen, and a little turned‑up nose. I can't imag‑ ine anything more lovely. If you're a bit vain, that's only to be expected with those good looks. Please enjoy the view my mirror provides; it was just envy that stopped me from offering it to you right away."

When the barber said this, horse‑laughs filled his shop. Meanwhile, our little lad stepped up to the mirror to look at himself, and tears filled his eyes. "Of course you didn't recognize your own Jacob, dear mother," he said to him‑ self. "He looked nothing like this in the happy days when you used to show him off to people." His eyes were now as tiny as pigs' eyes; his nose was a monster that hung down to his chin. His neck seemed to have disappeared, for his head grew right out of his shoulders. That's why it hurt so much to turn it to either side. His body was no bigger than it had been seven years ago when he was twelve, but over the years he had grown in width the way other boys grow in height before they are twenty. His back and chest bulged like a little, overfilled sack. This fat upper body sat on weak, short legs that hardly seemed strong enough to carry the burden. But his arms were fully grown and hung down his body. They were the size of a man's, with coarse, brownish‑ yellow hands that ended in long, spidery fingers. When he

stretched these out he could touch the floor without bending. That was how young Jacob looked: he had been turned
into a repulsive dwarf.

He now thought back to that morning when the old
woman had first stood in front of his mother's market baskets. Everything about her that he had mocked – the long
nose, the ugly fingers – she had given them all to him. She
had left out only the long, wobbly neck.

"Well, have you admired yourself enough for today,
my prince?" the barber asked as he approached Jacob and
looked at him scornfully. "I must say that if I had to come
up with something in my nightmares, it would never be as
funny-looking as you. But let me make a suggestion, my little friend. My barber shop has regular customers, but lately,
fewer than I would like. The reason is that my neighbor,
the barber Suds, found a giant somewhere to attract customers to his place. Well, let's face it, giants aren't all that
rare. A funny little man like you, that's something else.
Come, work for me and you shall have a place to live, food,
drink, and clothing. It's all yours for just standing outside
my door and inviting people to come in. If you like, you can
then whip up lather and hand the customers towels. I'm
sure we'll get along fine. I'll get more customers than the
barber with the giant, and you'll get tips from everybody."

Jacob was privately outraged at the suggestion that he

should serve as a lure to attract customers into the shop. Yet, he had no choice but to endure this insult without protest. So he told the barber quietly that he had no time for such tasks, and out he went.

Although the sorceress had ruined Jacob's looks, she had not spoiled his spirit. He sensed this himself, for he no longer thought and felt as he had seven years ago. In fact, he had become wiser and more considerate. He did not lament his lost beauty or bemoan his ugly body, but only felt sad because his own parents hadn't recognized him. So he decided to try again with his mother.

He approached her calmly in the marketplace and begged her to listen to what he had to say. He reminded her of the day when he, Jacob, had gone with the old woman; he reminded her of all sorts of specific events from his childhood. Then he told her how he had served the sorceress as a squirrel for seven years, and how she had bewitched him for having made fun of her. The shoemaker's wife did not know what to think. Everything he told her about his childhood was true, but her reaction to the story that he had been a squirrel for seven years was, "It's impossible. There are no such things as sorceresses." When she looked at him, he seemed so ugly that she could not believe this to be her beautiful son. Finally, she decided to discuss the matter with her husband. Gathering up her baskets, she told Jacob to come with her to the shoemaker's shop.

"Look at this, will you?" she said to her husband. "This person claims he is our lost Jacob. He told me how he was stolen seven years ago and put under a spell by a sorceress."

"Is that so?" the shoemaker interrupted. "Is that what he told you? Just wait, you rascal! I sent him away an hour ago, and now he's trying to trick you. So you were put under a spell, were you, sonny? Well, just hold on a moment while I remove it!" Then he went after Jacob with a bunch of belts and beat him on his back and arms so hard that the little fellow cried in pain and ran away.

In that city, like every other city, there were few people kind enough to help an unfortunate person who looked a bit ridiculous. So the unhappy dwarf spent the day without food or drink, and passed the night on the hard stone steps of a church.

When the first rays of the sun awakened him the next morning, he truly wondered how he was going to survive being rejected by both his mother and his father. He felt too proud ever to make a living as an object of curiosity, or let the barber earn money by having people gawk at him. What was he to do? Then he remembered that in his days as a squirrel he had acquired some skill as a cook. As a matter of fact, he thought he could probably hold his own against any chef, so he decided to put his talent to work.

As the streets grew crowded with the morning's business, he entered the church and said his prayers. Then he
went on his way. The duke of this land was a famous gourmet who loved a fine table and hired his cooks from all
corners of the world. Jacob now made his way to the ducal
palace. At the outer gate, the guards, of course, had some
fun with him, but he asked to see the head chef. Snicker-
ing, they led him to the inner courtyard where the other
servants stopped in their tracks to laugh at him. By and by,
a throng of palace servants crowded up the stairs. The
grooms and stable boys dropped their curry combs, the
pages rushed as fast as they could, the carpet spreaders for-
got to beat their carpets – everybody gathered around as if
an enemy were at the gates. The cry of "A dwarf, a dwarf!
Have you seen the dwarf?" filled the air.

The duke's chief steward appeared at the palace door.
He had a fierce expression and carried a huge whip. "In the
name of heaven, what is all this noise? Don't you know
that your lord is still sleeping?" He cracked the whip roughly
on the backs of a few stable boys and doorkeepers. "Master,"
they cried, "don't you see? We're bringing a dwarf, the fun-
niest you have ever seen." The chief steward forced himself
not to burst out laughing when he saw the little man, for
he feared that laughter would damage his dignity. So he
drove the others away with his whip, led Jacob inside, and

asked him his business. When he heard of Jacob's wish to see the head chef, he replied, "You're mistaken, little fellow. You're looking for me, the chief steward. You seek a position as the duke's personal dwarf, do you not?"

"No sir," the dwarf answered. "I am an experienced and talented cook and can make all sorts of rare dishes. If you would bring me to the head chef, perhaps he could put my skill to good use."

"As you wish, little fellow, but you are making a mistake. Kitchen work? As the duke's personal dwarf you would have had no work, and plenty to eat and drink as well as fine clothes. But we'll see. I doubt that you have as much skill as any of my master's cooks, and you're much too funny to be a kitchen boy." With these words the chief steward took him by the hand and led him to the chambers of the duke's head chef.

"Gracious sir," said the dwarf, bowing until his nose brushed the carpet, "do you need a clever cook?"

The head chef looked Jacob up and down before breaking onto a loud laugh and saying, "What? You – a cook? Do you think our stoves are so low that you can see their tops by standing on your toes and forcing your head out of your shoulders? Little man, whoever sent you here to seek work as a cook was mocking you." The head chef laughed heartily. So did the overseer and all the servants.

But the dwarf persisted. "What does an egg or two matter when you have plenty in the house, or a little flour, spice, and syrup, for that matter?" he asked. "Let me prepare a delicious dish for your master. Fetch me what I need, and before your eyes it shall be done so quickly that you'll say: he's a fine cook, all right, who does everything perfectly." It was wonderful to see how Jacob's little eyes shone when he talked, how his long nose wagged back and forth, and how he gestured with his long, bony fingers. "All right then," cried the head chef, taking the chief steward by the arm. "Just for fun, let's go to the kitchen."

They went through several rooms and corridors and finally reached the kitchen. This was a large, spacious building across from the palace. It was magnificently furnished with twenty stoves where fires burned constantly. A stream of fresh water, home to many fishes, flowed right through the middle. The provisions were stored in cupboards of marble and precious wood. To the right and left, ten rooms contained everything that all the lands of Europe and the Orient could offer to please the palate. Kitchen servants with forks and spoons ran around. Pans and kettles rattled everywhere. When the head chef entered, the whole staff stood at attention, so still that only the crackling fires and rushing water could be heard.

"What has the duke ordered for breakfast this morning?" the head chef asked an old cook who was First Break-fast Maker.

"Sir, he desires a Danish soup and hamburger dumplings."

"Good," said the head chef, "did you hear what our Master wants for breakfast? Do you trust yourself to make these difficult dishes? I know you'll never get the dump-lings right. That's a secret recipe."

"Nothing easier," replied the dwarf to everyone's astonishment, for he had often cooked these things when he was a squirrel. "Nothing easier. For the soup I'll need this and that spice, the fat of a wild boar, seasonings, and eggs. But for the dumplings," – and here he lowered his voice so only the head chef and the First Breakfast Maker could hear him, "I'll need four kinds of meat, some wine, goose fat, ginger, and an herb they call stomach cheer."

"Ha, by Saint Benedict! What sorcerer taught you all this?" cried the First Breakfast Maker, amazed. You have described it all down to a hair, and we didn't even know about the herb. That should make it even better. You are a miracle of a cook!"

"I would never have thought this," said the head chef. "Let him try his hand at breakfast. Give him what he needs – pots, pans, everything."

The kitchen staff followed this order and prepared

everything on the stove. But the dwarf could not reach that high, so they put two chairs together and placed a marble slab across these so the little miracle-maker could begin to work his marvels. The chefs, kitchen boys, and servants formed a large circle around Jacob and watched in awe as he moved with speed and precision, preparing the dishes neatly and elegantly. When he had finished the preparation, he ordered both bowls to be placed on the fire to cook until he called out. Then he counted: one, two, three – all the way up to five hundred. "Stop!" he cried. "Remove the pots." Then he invited the head chef to taste the result.

The head chef asked for a golden spoon, which a kitchen boy washed in the stream and handed to him. Then he went to the stove very ceremoniously, tried the dishes Jacob had cooked, closed his eyes, and licked his lips. "Delicious, by my Lord's life, delicious! Won't you try a spoonful as well, Head Steward? The steward bowed, took the spoon, tried the food, and was overcome with delight. "All honor to your art, sir, you are an experienced cook, but you have never made the soup or the hamburger dumplings as wonderfully as this." The First Breakfast Maker now savored it himself and shook the dwarf's hand respectfully, saying, "Little fellow, you are a master of your craft. Yes, this stomach cheer gives everything a fascinating flavor."

At that moment the duke's chamberlain appeared to report that his master desired breakfast. The food was placed on silver platters and sent to the duke while the head kitchen chef took the dwarf into his room for a chat. They were only there for the time it takes to say half the Lord's Prayer when a messenger summoned the head chef to the duke. The head chef followed after putting on his best clothes.

The duke looked very pleased. He had devoured everything on the silver platters and was wiping his beard when the head chef entered. "Listen," he said, "I have always been satisfied with my cooks, but you must tell me who prepared my breakfast this morning. It has never been this good for as long as I have sat on the throne of my fathers. Tell me this chef's name. I wish to send him a few ducats as a present."

"My Lord, this is a strange story," the head chef answered, and told how a dwarf had been brought to him this morning asking to become a cook, and how everything else had happened. Amazed, the duke asked to have the dwarf brought before him. When he asked Jacob who he was and where he came from, of course Jacob could not say that he had been placed under a spell or that he had lived as a squirrel before this. But he did tell the truth when he said that he now had neither mother nor father and that he had learned to cook from an old woman. The duke asked

no more questions, but took pleasure in the funny appear‑
ance of his brilliant new cook.

"Do you wish to stay here with me?" he asked. "If so, I
shall give you fifty ducats a year, fine clothes, and in addi‑
tion, two pairs of trousers. For this you must prepare my
breakfast every day, teach the other cooks how to make the
noon meal, and then look after my kitchen in general. Be‑
cause everyone in my palace receives a name from me, I
shall call you Longnose and you shall have all the dignities
of a First Assistant Chef. Dwarf Longnose fell down before
the mighty duke, kissed his feet, and promised to serve
him faithfully.

Jacob was now well taken care of and he fulfilled his
duties honorably. One could say that the duke became an
entirely different man once Dwarf Longnose began to serve
him. In the past he used to throw plates and dishes at his
kitchen staff. Once he threw an undercooked calf's foot at
his head chef, hitting him in the forehead so hard that the
man fell down and had to stay in bed for three days. The
duke would make amends with handfuls of ducats, but still
no chef dared bring him food without quaking and trem‑
bling in fear. Since the dwarf had come to the palace, how‑
ever, things seemed magically changed. In order to savor
the art of his smallest servant, the duke ate five times a day
instead of three. What was more, his face never showed dis‑

content. No, he found everything new and inspired; he was convivial, pleasant – and grew fatter every day.

In the middle of the meal he often called for Dwarf Longnose and his head chef. Seating them at his right and his left hand, he would feed them bits of delicious food with his own fingers – a gesture they both appreciated.

The dwarf was the wonder of the city. People begged permission from the head chef to watch him cook. The duke even let some of the noblest gentlemen send their cooks to take lessons from Dwarf Longnose. This brought in good money, for each paid half a ducat per day. In order to keep the rest of the cooks happy and prevent any envy, Dwarf Longnose gave them the money that the noblemen paid for these lessons. For almost two years he lived this life of affluence and honor, troubled only by the lingering thought of his parents.

Life continued like this with no surprises, until a very strange thing happened. Dwarf Longnose was particularly skillful and lucky in buying food for the duke. When he had time, he often went himself to the market to buy poultry and fruit. One morning he went to find a fat goose of the sort the duke loved. These days when he walked up and down inspecting the fare at the market, his appearance commanded respect rather than scorn. People recognized him as the duke's famous chef and the goose girls were happy when he turned his long nose in their direction.

At the far end of one row of stalls, he spied a woman who had geese to sell but was not hawking her wares to the crowd. He went over to her and took stock of her geese. They met with his approval and he bought three in their cage. He loaded the cage onto his broad shoulders and headed home. He thought it odd that only two of the birds were honking and screeching like normal geese. The third sat quietly and moaned. Then it heaved a sigh like a human being. "That one is half sick," he muttered. "I'd better kill it as soon as I get home so I can start to prepare it." To his shock, the goose answered in a loud, clear voice:

> *Try to stab me if you dare,*
> *First I'll bite you, that I swear.*
> *Try to choke me, are you brave?*
> *I'll bring you to an early grave.*

Dwarf Longnose set the cage down in shock and stared at the goose. The goose stared back at him with beautiful, intelligent eyes and sighed. "For pity's sake," cried the dwarf, "can you speak, Miss Goose? I wouldn't have believed it. Do not be afraid! I won't let anything happen to such a rare bird. I'll bet that you have not always worn these feathers. I can tell because I myself was once a common squirrel."

"You are right," the goose answered, "when you say I

was not born in this shameful form. When I was a baby in my cradle no one guessed that I, Mimi, daughter of the great sorcerer Wetterbock, would end up slaughtered in the duke's kitchen."

"Be calm, dear Miss Mimi," the dwarf reassured her. "I am an honorable fellow and First Assistant Chef of His Grace the Duke. I promise, nobody will wring your pretty neck. I'll make you a special pen in my own quarters and feed you myself. In my free time I shall entertain you. I'll tell the other cooks that I am fattening you up with special herbs for the duke's table, and as soon as I can, I'll set you free."

The goose thanked him through her tears. And the dwarf did as he had promised. He slaughtered the other two geese but built Mimi her own stall under the pretext of preparing her especially for the duke. He did not give her common feed, but rather baked goods and sweets. When he had free time, he came to talk with her and comfort her. They told each other their stories, which is how the dwarf learned that Mimi's father, a great sorcerer, lived on the isle of Gotland. He had quarreled with an old witch who won the argument by trickery and deception. As her revenge, the witch had turned Mimi into a goose and carried her far away to this place. When Dwarf Longnose told Mimi the story of his own life, she said, "I have some experience in these matters. My father gave my sisters and me some

instruction in the magic arts, at least as much as he was allowed to reveal. Your story of the dispute over your mother's spices and your transformation when you smelled a certain herb, even some of the old woman's words – all these tell me that she cast her spell over you with an herb, and that the right plant will release you from your spell." This was small comfort for Dwarf Longnose. How would he ever find the right herb? Still, he thanked her and tried to keep up hope.

At about this time a neighboring prince came to pay a state visit to the duke, who called Dwarf Longnose to him and said, "The time has come for you to prove you are my loyal servant and true master of your craft. Aside from me, this prince is the finest gourmet in the land, a true connoisseur of food, and a wise man as well. You must see to it that when he dines at my table, his astonishment grows with every day. Do not risk my anger by serving any dish twice during his visit. My treasurer will give you whatever you need to accomplish all this. If you have to fry gold and diamonds in fat, then do so. I would rather be penniless than embarrassed in front of this prince."

When the duke finished speaking, the dwarf bowed low and answered, "It will be as you wish, my Lord. God willing, I shall please the fine palate of this prince."

And so the little cook drew upon all his art. He did

not spare his master's treasury. All day long you could see him amidst clouds of fire and smoke. His voice echoed through the kitchen as he ordered the kitchen boys and the lower cooks around. Now, I admit, I could be like those camel drivers of Aleppo who, when they tell their tales to travelers, always describe exquisite meals. They spin out details of every dish for as long as it takes to stimulate incredible hunger in their listeners, who finally break down and get out their finest food and have a meal with their camel drivers. But I'm not like that.

The visiting prince had been a guest of the duke for two weeks, living in bliss and splendor. They ate no fewer than five times a day, and the duke was delighted with the skill of Dwarf Longnose, for he could read satisfaction on the face of his guest. On the fifteenth day the duke called the dwarf to the table to introduce him to the prince. He asked the prince whether he was satisfied with the dwarf.

"You are a wonderful cook," answered the visitor, "and you know what it means to eat well. In the entire time I have been here you have never served the same dish twice, and it was always presented magnificently. But tell me, why don't you bring out the queen of all cuisine: the Pâté Souzerain?

The dwarf was shocked, for this was a queen he had never heard of. Nonetheless, he composed himself and answered, "My Lord, I had hoped that your presence would grace this court for a long time to come, so I decided to wait with this dish, for how else should the cook mark the day of your departure from us than with the queen of pâtés?"

"Is that so?" the duke replied with a laugh. "And were you waiting for me to die before you served it to me? I have never yet tasted this dish, so think of a different farewell gesture, for tomorrow you must serve us the pâté."

"As you wish, my Lord," answered the dwarf, and went away. But he did not go cheerfully. He knew that his day of disgrace and misery had finally come. You see, he did not know how to make pâtés. Therefore, he went to his room to cry over his fate. Mimi the goose, who had free run of his room, came to him and asked why he wept. "Dry your tears," she said, when she heard of the Pâté Souzerain, "We often had this at my father's table. I am fairly sure I know what you need for it. You take a little of this and a little of that, and even if you haven't got everything, the gentlemen won't have such keen palates to notice if something is missing.

The dwarf jumped for joy at Mimi's words and blessed the day he bought the goose. Then he began to prepare the queen of all pâtés. First he made a small test portion. It tasted wonderful. When the head chef tasted a bit, he praised Dwarf Longnose for expanding his range as a cook.

The next day, the dwarf made a whole recipe of the pâté. While it was still warm from the oven, he decorated it with a wreath of flowers and sent it to the duke's table. He dressed in his finest clothes and went to the dining room where the first carver was busy serving pieces of the pâté on a silver spatula to the duke and his guest. The duke bit into his piece with gusto, rolled his eyes heavenwards, and said when he had swallowed, "Ah, ah, ah! Now I know why this is called the queen of all pâtés, but my dwarf is also the king of all cooks. Wouldn't you say so, dear friend?"

The guest took a teeny bite, savored it carefully in his mouth, and smiled a slightly caustic, mysterious smile. "The thing is very nicely made," he said pushing away his plate. "But it is not quite a Souzerain. I thought as much."

The duke furrowed his brow in distress and blushed in shame. "You dog of a dwarf," he cried, "You dare to do this to your lord? Shall I cut off your head as punishment for your poor cooking?"

"Master, by heaven, I prepared this dish as perfectly as I could. I cannot imagine what might be wrong with it," said the dwarf trembling in fear.

"That is a lie, you knave," the duke cried and kicked

Dwarf Longnose with his foot. "Had it been perfect, my guest would never found fault with it! I think I'll have *you* chopped up and baked in a pâté."

"Have pity," the little fellow cried and crawled over to the guest on his knees. Clasping the prince's feet, the dwarf said, "Tell me what was wrong with this dish that displeased your palate. Do not let me die for a handful of meat and flour."

"That won't help you, Longnose," the visitor answered with a laugh. "I knew yesterday that you would not be able to make this as well as my own cook. You lack a tiny herb that does not grow in this country. It has a strange name. They call it sneezer's joy. Without it, the pâté will never have the right flavor, so your master can never know the true pâté."

This infuriated the duke. "But I *will* have the true pâté," he bellowed, eyes blazing. "I swear by my honor, either you will have the pâté tomorrow correctly made, or the head of this servant will decorate my palace gate. Get out of here, you cur. You have twenty-four hours!"

When the duke had stopped shouting, Dwarf Longnose went to his room in tears. There he told the goose of his fate: he was doomed to die because he had never heard of this particular herb. "Is that all?" she said. "Then I can help you, for my father taught me all about plants and herbs. At any other time you would have risked death, but at the moment there is a new moon – just the time when the herb grows. But tell me, do any old chestnut trees grow around the palace?"

"Oh, yes," Longnose replied, a bit calmer, "There is a grove of chestnut trees two hundred paces from here on the shores of the lake. But why?"

"Your little herb blooms only at the base of old chest⁄nut trees," said Mimi. "Let's not waste time. We must go and look for what you need. Carry me there on your arm and put me down outside. I'll hunt for you."

He did as she advised and went to the door of the palace. Here the gatekeeper barred their way with his spear. "It's all over for you, Longnose," he said. "I have the strictest orders not to let you out of the palace."

"But surely I am allowed into the garden," the dwarf answered. "Be good enough to send someone to the First Steward to ask if I may look for herbs in the garden." This request was granted, for the garden had such high walls there was no chance of escape. Once outside, Longnose put Mimi on the ground, and she hurried toward the lake where the chestnut trees stood. He followed her with fear in his heart, for he knew this was his last and only hope. He had made up his mind: if he didn't find the herb, he would throw himself into the lake rather than be exe⁄cuted. The goose hunted frantically, turning over every blade of grass with her bill. She found nothing. Finally, out of pity and fear, she began to cry, for the sun was setting and it was becoming very difficult to see anything.

At that moment the dwarf glanced across the lake and called out, "Look, look, there on the far side of the lake. I see a tall, old tree. Let's go over there and try our luck." The goose hopped and flew ahead while the dwarf ran as fast as his short legs could carry him. This chestnut tree cast such a long, deep shadow that you could hardly see anything beneath it. Suddenly, the goose stood stock still, flapped her wings in joy, darted with her head into the tall grass, and plucked something that she handed to the astonished dwarf. "This is the herb. There is plenty growing here so you will have enough."

The dwarf studied the plant. Its sweet aroma greeted his nostrils, reminding him of the scene of his transformation. Its leaves and stem were bluish green and it bore a red flower with a yellow border.

"God be praised!" he cried out. "What a miracle! Do you know, I think this is the herb that changed me from a squirrel into this horrible shape I have now. Shall I try it?"

"Not yet," begged the goose. "Take a handful of this herb with you and let's return to your room and put together all your money and belongings. Then we can try the herb's power."

They did all this and the little dwarf's anticipation was so keen that the sound of his heartbeat filled the room. Once he had made a bundle with the fifty or sixty ducats he had saved, along with some clothes and shoes, he said. "Now, if it please God, let me cast off this affliction." So saying, he stuck his nose into the herbs and breathed in deeply. Suddenly, all his joints and limbs cracked and he felt his head lift up from his shoulders. He stared at his nose, which shrank smaller and smaller while his chest and back flattened out and his legs got longer.

The goose watched in amazement. "Look how big and handsome you are," she cried. "Thank God there's nothing left of your old shape!" Jacob, who was pleased to hear this, folded his hands and prayed. But his joy did not make him forget his debt to Mimi the goose. Despite a powerful urge to go find his parents, he said, "I have no one but you to thank that the spell has been lifted. Without you I would never have found the herb and might have died under the headsman's axe. I hope I can repay you. Let me take you to your father who is so versed in magic that he will surely know how to change you back to your true shape." The goose accepted his offer, weeping for joy. Jacob escaped from the palace with her unobserved and made his way to the coast in the direction of her homeland.

What else can I tell you – except that they completed

their journey, that the sorcerer Wetterbock removed the spell from his daughter, and sent Jacob on his way laden with gifts, though he promised to come back to Mimi as soon as he was able. Jacob returned to the city of his birth where his parents were overjoyed to see the handsome young man they recognized as their son. With the gifts he brought, they bought themselves a shop and became rich and happy.

I should add one more thing. After Dwarf Longnose had left the palace of the duke, there was much commotion, for on the following day when the duke went to fulfill his oath to execute the dwarf for not finding the right herb, the cook was nowhere to be found. His guest, the prince, accused him of spiriting the dwarf away so as not to deprive himself of his best chef. The duke stood accused of breaking his word and, as a result, the two leaders went to war against each other. This is known in history books as the Herb War. After many a battle, a treaty was finally signed, which became known as the "Peace of Pâté." At the reconciliation banquet, the prince's cook prepared a Pâté Souzerain, the queen of all pâtés, which the duke judged superb. Thus we see how the smallest causes often have great effects.
And that is the tale of
Dwarf Longnose.

◆ ◆
◆

About the Illustrator

Born near the Soviet-Korean border, Boris Pak (1935–1992) became a field geologist at the insistence of his father. He first found work near Leningrad, in the Northwest Geological Expedition, and at nights studied art at the Repin Institute of Painting, Sculpture, and Architecture. His work soon began to appear in national exhibitions and in newspapers and journals. After graduating, he went on to teach at the Gogol Artists' School. In addition to illustrations for numerous books, Pak created large-scale works for several buildings in the city of Almaty. He was awarded the honor of Distinguished Artist of the Kazakh SSR in 1989. His work is held in private collections and in museums in Moscow, Almaty & at Harvard University.

◆ ◆
◆